Traveling Animals

Written by Brylee Gibson

Rigby

Traveling Animals

Every year, some animals move from one place to another.

These animals move to:
- find food or water
- have babies or lay eggs
- find a warm place

Some animals move back to the place they left and some don't.

ant

aphids

arctic tern

eel

Fact Box

About 100 million red crabs live on Christmas Island.

red crabs

Every year, the red crabs of Christmas Island travel from the forest to the beach to have their babies. They move in a straight line, and climb over anything that is in their way. They have to travel in the morning or in the evening, when it is not too hot, or they could die.

Key
- crabs
- rainforest

Christmas Island is north-west of Australia.

These bugs are called aphids.
Aphids make a sweet juice that ants like to eat.
But the aphids need food to make the juice.

aphids

The ants carry the aphids in their mouth.

ant

aphid

Aphids get their food from the trees and grass. But the aphids do not get there by themselves. These ants carry the aphids.

eel

Eels live in ponds and rivers,
but when they want to lay their eggs,
they swim to the ocean.
When their eggs are laid, the eels go away,
but nobody knows where.
When baby eels hatch, they swim back to the
ponds and rivers that their parents came from.

① The adult eels swim from the river to the ocean.

② The adult eels lay their eggs in the ocean.

③ The eel eggs hatch.

④ The baby eels swim back to the river.

baby eel

Every year, these butterflies
will go from their home to a warmer place.
Some butterflies fly from one country to another,
until they find a warm place.
They can fly for hours without stopping.
The butterflies will go back to their home
when it gets warm again.

Monarch butterflies

11

arctic terns

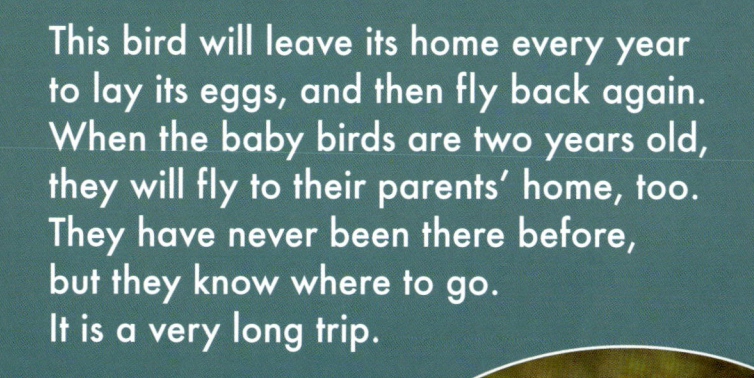

This bird will leave its home every year
to lay its eggs, and then fly back again.
When the baby birds are two years old,
they will fly to their parents' home, too.
They have never been there before,
but they know where to go.
It is a very long trip.

springbok

These springbok live in dry lands.
When there is no water for them to drink,
they must move to another place.
They all move at the same time in a big group.
Sometimes there are so many in the group
that other animals can get crushed.

15

earthworm

Most animals travel north or south,
but earthworms travel up and down.
In autumn, some earthworms will dig deep
into the earth and stay there for the winter.
In spring, when the earth is warm again,
they will travel back up to the top of the ground.

Animals that travel...

to find food or water

to have babies or lay eggs

to find a warm place

Index

aphids..................6–7

birds 13

butterflies 10

earthworms 17

eels..................... 8

red crabs........... 5

springbok 14

Guide Notes

Title: Traveling Animals
Stage: Launching Fluency – Orange

Genre: Nonfiction
Approach: Guided Reading
Processes: Thinking Critically, Exploring Language, Processing Information
Written and Visual Focus: Labels, Index, Caption, Fact Box, Map, Key, Life Cycle Diagram
Word Count: 381

THINKING CRITICALLY
(sample questions)
- What do you know about animals that travel from place to place?
- What might you expect to see in this book?
- Look at the index. Encourage the students to think about the information and make predictions about the text content.
- Look at pages 4 and 5. What could be a problem for the people who live in the path of the crabs?
- Look at the pictures on pages 6 and 7. How do you think the ants get the sweet juice from the aphids?
- Look at pages 8 and 9. Why do you think nobody knows where the eels go after they have laid their eggs?
- Look at pages 10 and 11. How do you think butterflies can fly for hours without stopping?
- Look at pages 12 and 13. How do you think the baby birds know where to go?

EXPLORING LANGUAGE

Terminology
Photograph credits, index

Vocabulary
Clarify: aphids, hatch, autumn
Singular/Plural: animal/animals, egg/eggs, tree/trees
Homonyms: one/won, to/two/too, their/there

Print Conventions
Apostrophes – possessive (parents'), contraction (don't); colon